MW01101191

# Barbie at the Olympic Games

# Barbie at the Olympic Games

A story by
**Geneviève Schurer**

Illustrations by
**Liliane Crismer**

First published by Hemma Publications 1993
English edition published by Hinkler Books Pty Ltd 2004
17-23 Redwood Drive
Dingley VIC 3172 Australia
www.hinklerbooks.com

ISBN 1 7412 1769 5
Edited by Juile Haydon
Printed & bound in Australia

# Contents

## Chapter 1

# On the rink

Wearing her rollerblades, Julia glides and whirls around the rink. The floor is made of wood. As the rollerblades touch the smooth, shining floor, they make almost no noise. The only sound that can be heard is a soft whoosh.

It is a training session, and Julia is dressed in a pretty mauve leotard. The leotard has a small skirt. Julia has tied her long brown hair up high on her head. Her thick hair looks like a horse's mane. On her feet, she is wearing white boots made from leather. The boots extend high up her calves. Her face is illuminated by a magnificent smile, which gives the false impression that skating is easy.

Leaning against the railing that surrounds the rink, Barbie

admires her friend's skill. For the moment, Julia is alone on the rink. Sitting not so far away on a bench, Miss Koper, her skating coach, observes her with a critical eye.

'Your arms need to be more supple, Julia!' Miss Koper calls

out. 'They are too stiff when you lift them over your head.'

Julia follows her coach's instructions, then spins on the spot and curtsies.

Barbie applauds enthusiastically. 'Superb, Julia! You've made incredible progress.'

'There's still a lot more to do,' Miss Koper says stiffly. 'Only the best can compete at the Olympic Games.'

'Julia will be the best, Miss Koper,' Barbie says. 'I'm quite sure of that.'

'We'll see, Barbie. We'll see,' Miss Koper says.

When Julia approaches the railing, Barbie hands her a pink towel, which the young skater wraps around her neck.

'You can take a break, Julia,' says her coach. 'We'll begin training again in fifteen minutes. You can join us, Barbie, if you have your rollerblades. I know you're a very good skater, and a little exercise never hurt anyone.'

'Gosh, Julia, it mustn't be much fun having such a grumpy coach,' Barbie whispers in Julia's ear, as soon as the two young women are alone.

'It's true that Miss Koper grumbles a lot,' Julia says, 'but deep down, she has a heart of gold. She just wants everything to be perfect.'

'Excuse me, Miss,' a little voice says from behind our friends. 'Can you tell me what kind of skates you're wearing?'

Julia and Barbie turn to look at the owner of the voice. They see a pretty young girl, who looks about twelve years old. She has a cute button nose and freckles, and she is watching them both curiously.

'Your skates don't look like roller skates,' the little girl says.

Julia smiles and leans over towards the girl. 'My skates are rollerblades. Roller skates have four wheels, two in the front and two in the back. Rollerblades have four wheels in a line. Because of this, rollerbladers can do the same sorts of moves as ice skaters. We can dance, we can spin around, we can leap. But we don't need ice to skate on. We can skate almost anywhere. It's very practical.'

'Are you going to compete in the Olympic Games with these strange skates? I heard the older lady say something about it,' the little girl asks.

'Yes, rollerbladers, like me, have been invited to the Olympic Games to participate in a demonstration. That's a competition that's just for show. Maybe one day rollerblading will be an official Olympic sport, but at the moment, it's not. But, going in the demonstration means that I'll be up against the best rollerbladers in the world, and my coach, Miss Koper, wants me to win the gold medal. That's why she's pushing me so hard. I must confess that I'm a little nervous.'

## Chapter 2

# After the training session

Wrapped in big fluffy towels, Barbie and Julia step out of the shower room. Through the wall, they can hear dozens of feet stepping in time to loud music.

There is a gymnasium next door and an aerobics class has just started. Barbie and Julia are tired after their training session with Miss Koper. Barbie had her rollerblades with her, so she joined Julia for the session. It was hard work! They were both relieved when the session ended and Miss Koper sent them to the showers.

As the young women get dressed and put on their make-up, they chat happily.

'Next time, I'll bring Skipper,' Barbie says. 'I'd like to see how well she survives one of Miss Koper's training sessions.'

'I have to train even harder,' Julia says. 'Miss Koper wants me to be in top shape for the Olympic Games.'

'You're already in great shape,' Barbie reassures her. 'We just did the sort of workout that an elite athlete would do, and you breezed through it.'

'You're in pretty good shape, too. If I were Miss Koper, I'd add you to the team.'

'Hey, don't even joke about it!' Barbie says, laughing. 'It's my job to support you and keep you motivated. That's what friends are for. I can keep you company while you train, but I haven't been training hard enough to compete with the best rollerbladers in the world.'

'You could start training now,' Julia urges. 'There's still time. I'd love you to be my team-mate. I'd feel more confident if you were on the team.'

'No,' Barbie says, smiling. 'There's no way I'm going to spend my days in the company of Miss Koper. I don't think I have as much patience as you do.'

The door opens and Skipper walks in. 'Hello, girls! It looked like you both had a great workout. They say that talent and nerves of steel are the two secret ingredients of champions. I think you both have that.'

'Skipper!' Barbie says. 'We didn't see you arrive!'

'I arrived a while ago and watched you train. I hid at the

back so you wouldn't see me and rope me into exercising. I'm tired from just watching you two!'

'Do you think that a person becomes an athlete by sitting in front of the TV and eating popcorn all day?' Julia asks, with a smile.

'I know, I know,' Skipper agrees. 'You've got to work hard so that you have a strong body and mind, but I also know that I'm quite incapable of working that hard. I admire athletes like you very much.'

'Well, you can admire us while we go and get an iced chocolate. I'm thirsty. Do you want to join us?' Julia asks.

'Yes,' Skipper says. 'I want to talk to you about a wonderful idea that I've had. You two are future champions. You're both cute and talented. So why don't I organise some sort of fan club to support you? Don't worry, you'll be able to leave all the organising up to me.'

## Chapter 3

# A meeting

The large auditorium is full of athletes and their friends. They are talking in low murmurs. All the athletes have been officially selected to represent their country at the Olympic Games. There is a platform at the front of the auditorium. A long table with twelve chairs is on the platform. There are microphones set up on the table.

The organisers of the Olympic team sit down at the table. They have set up this meeting to explain how the individual sports are organised at the Games and to respond to questions from the athletes. They begin by showing everyone in the auditorium the symbol of the Olympic Games: the interlocking rings. They explain that each ring represents a continent: black for Africa, blue for Europe, green for Australia, yellow for Asia, and red for the Americas. On a large screen, they show photographs of the host country and the Olympic Village. The athletes see the pools, tracks, fields, rinks and gymnasiums where they will be competing.

When the presentation is over, the officials ask if there are any questions. People raise their hands.

'Can we try out the tracks and pools before the actual competition begins?'

'Yes. You will arrive several days before the Games begin, and you'll be able to train in the venues where you will be competing.'

There are several more questions before Fred, the greedy shot-put champion, asks, 'Do they know how to make good pizza in the host country?'

Now that the serious stuff is over, everyone in the auditorium suddenly relaxes. People begin to chat to their neighbours.

'If you have no further questions,' an official says into his microphone, 'we will end the meeting. You are all invited to come into the foyer for refreshments.'

Everyone moves towards the foyer.

'Barbie, Julia, come here!' Skipper calls, waving her arm so that Barbie and Julia will see amongst the crowd. 'I want to introduce you to my friend

Fanny. She's a gymnast. She's going to win lots of medals at the Games.'

'I've seen Julia training with Miss Koper,' Fanny says, smiling. 'I think you're a wonderful rollerblader.'

'Hello, everyone,' says a tall brunette with cropped hair. 'My name's Lisa. I'm a diver. I'm very pleased to meet you. It'll be great to be surrounded by friends at the Olympic Games. It'll help us deal with our nerves.'

'Well, all for one, and one for all!' Barbie says. The five young

women link hands and swear to support each other throughout the Olympic Games.

## Chapter 4

# The fall

On the stadium seating that surrounds the skating rink, a happy group of boys and girls huddle together. They are members of Julia and Barbie's fan club. Skipper has done a wonderful job of organising the group of fans to support Julia and Barbie while they train.

Julia and Barbie are roller-blading on the rink to music. Julia executes a tricky move and the young men and women stand and whistle. They wave

coloured banners around as they applaud.

The first time the fan club gathered, Miss Koper felt a little agitated. She was worried that the noise would disturb her students' concentration. However, she soon noticed that Julia and Barbie were doing more complicated moves in front of their fans. 'I suppose the Olympic Games is a public competition,' Miss Koper said to herself. 'It's not a bad thing for the girls to get used to an unruly crowd.' The fans haven't missed any of the training sessions. Both

Julia and Barbie have become accustomed to their cheers.

'Super! Wonderful!' Skipper cries.

'Yes! Yes!' the members of the fan club cry, each time Julia and Barbie perform a move.

'Julia! Barbie!' the fans chant, in time with the music and the rollerbladers' moves.

The next morning, there are fewer fans than usual around the rink. But those who are there are so noisy they make up for their absent friends.

'Okay, Julia, we'll try that

again,' Miss Koper calls. 'As soon as you pick up a bit of speed, you've got to bend your legs in order to balance as you spin. Again!'

Patiently, Julia gets back into position. It's the tenth time that she's had to perform this difficult manoeuvre this morning. She says

nothing, but she is feeling a little tired. She wishes she could work on a less intricate move. She flashes a brave smile at Barbie as she begins to speed up to do the move. The fans watch avidly. As she reaches the necessary speed, Julia bends her knees the way that Miss Koper instructed her to. She flows into a backwards step in order to start forming the spiral. Suddenly, without any apparent reason, her foot slides a little and her leg buckles. Julia cries out as she falls hard on her back.

The members of her fan club stand up, shocked. Miss Koper

and Barbie rush towards Julia, who is lying on the floor of the rink. She doesn't move, but her eyes are filling with tears. She doesn't seem able to speak.

'Julia, Julia, answer me. Are you badly hurt?' Barbie asks, kneeling by her friend.

'Julia, please speak,' Miss Koper says, suddenly becoming tender and sweet.

'Don't move her,' says a red-haired boy with a worried look on his face. 'Someone has gone to call an ambulance. She's probably in shock, but that will pass.'

Barbie takes her friend's hand. 'We're all here for you, Julia. Don't worry. We'll look after you.'

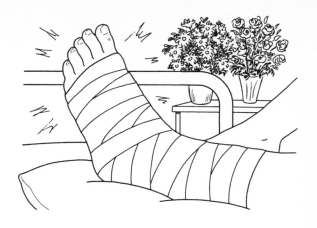

## Chapter 5

# Julia's room

There are so many flowers in Julia's room it's as though her bed is positioned in the middle of a garden. Wrapped in thick, white bandages, the young woman's left foot looks like a soft toy. One arm is also hidden under a pile of bandages.

'So, how are your injuries today?' Barbie asks, as she moves in to kiss her friend's forehead. 'You really gave us all a fright, you know. It was shocking to see you unable to speak.'

'The doctor explained that the fall knocked the air out of my lungs,' Julia says. 'I couldn't speak because I had no breath.'

'I know that you haven't hurt your arm too badly, but what did the doctor say about your ankle?'

'I've torn a muscle. The doctor doesn't know how long I'll be out of action. I'm really worried about it. Everyone is being lovely, but I wish I knew whether I'll be able to compete in the Olympic Games.'

'Julia, my child, how are you?' Miss Koper says, as she enters Julia's room with a big, fluffy teddy bear in her arms. 'I've brought you a little companion to talk to while you recover. He can be the team's mascot, if you like. Perhaps he can come with us to the Olympic Games.'

'Are you sure that I'll be

going?' Julia asks in a low, anguished voice.

'Of course! After a couple of weeks of rest and some physiotherapy, you'll be as good as new. This accident will be nothing more than a bad memory.'

'Are you sure?' Julia asks.

'Because if it's true, I swear to you that I will do all that I can to get back into shape. Even this teddy bear will be proud of me.'

'Listen, Julia,' Miss Koper says, 'we all want you to recover as quickly as possible, but your recovery depends on how strong

and brave you can be. While your doctor will help you as much as she can, how well you recover is mainly up to you.'

'My physiotherapist, Christine, has already come to see me. She's adorable. I can't wait to start training with her. I've promised her that I will do my best. I don't want all the rollerblading training that I've done over the years to come to nothing.'

'Julia,' Barbie says, 'don't think bad thoughts. You will go to the Olympic Games. I'm certain of that.'

Just then Skipper steps

through the door. 'Hi, Julia! Today I've just come by myself, because I imagine you need some peace and quiet, but tomorrow all your fans are coming to show their support.'

'I'll leave you with Skipper. I'll be back soon,' says Barbie.

'I'll be back soon as well,' Miss Koper adds.

'Thank you for the teddy bear, Miss Koper. I think I'll call him Jo. What do you think?'

'That's a great name,' Miss Koper agrees.

In the corridor, Miss Koper touches Barbie's arm. 'I've got to

talk to you. Have you got a
moment?'

'Of course. Is it serious?'

'Yes, a little. In order not to
worry Julia, I've been very optimistic when I speak to her. But
the truth is that her injury may
take a long time to heal. Julia

may not be able to compete in the Olympic Games.'

Barbie gasps. 'Julia will be so sad! She has trained so hard.'

'I'm sad, too,' Miss Koper says, 'but my task is to make sure that there is someone who can fill her position in the competition if Julia can't make it. Barbie, I need you to be ready to take Julia's place.'

Barbie is stunned. 'Me?'

'Yes. You've got to learn a rollerblading routine. The whole country is counting on you. You can't let us down.'

At this point, just as Julia lost her voice when she fell, Barbie loses hers. She is speechless!

## Chapter 6

# Barbie's training

Concentrating hard, Barbie skates around the rink. She has dropped everything to prepare for the Olympics, in case her friend cannot compete.

This morning, Julia has come to the rink on crutches. To encourage Barbie, she gives her some advice and admires how well she is progressing. 'I'm thrilled! You're skating like a champion. Miss Koper must be really pleased with how you're coming along.'

'If she's happy with me, she doesn't show it,' Barbie whispers into her friend's ear. 'She always seems to be in a terrible mood.'

Julia bursts out laughing. 'No way! You just don't know her well enough yet. She is grumpy, but she's got a heart of gold. I imagine she's very proud of you.'

'Barbie, are you ready to go?' Miss Koper yells from the other end of the rink. 'You'll have time to chat after you've finished your training. There isn't much left to do now.'

As she listens to Miss Koper's instructions, Barbie turns towards

her friend. The young women are suddenly overcome with a mad laughter. 'You're right, Julia. She must be very pleased with my progress if she speaks to me like that.'

Julia sits down and Barbie moves into the centre of the rink.

She starts to practise a pirouette, her best move.

'Your arms need to be higher!' Miss Koper yells. 'Higher! Lift your hands!'

That afternoon at the medical centre, Julia has a rehabilitation session with Christine, her physiotherapist. Two other women join in the session. They are Anne, who fractured her leg in a motorcycle accident, and Meg, who fell while skiing. The three convalescents have been unable to do much exercise since their accidents. They all want to be able to walk and play sport properly once more.

Christine takes them through some gentle exercises. Slowly, the women feel their bodies growing stronger, though they have a long way to go before they are completely recovered.

'Hey, Christine, look! My leg is getting better. I can bend my knee,' Anne exclaims.

'That's marvellous! Try to do it a few more times. How about you, Julia? How are your exercises going? That's it! Good, now begin again. You're doing really well.'

Feeling greatly encouraged by Christine, the young women stretch their limbs.

'Okay,' Christine calls, 'that's it for today. We don't want to overdo it. Well done!'

## Chapter 7

# The boys' support

As soon as the doorbell rings, Barbie leaps out of the shower. She wraps herself in a pink dressing gown and ties a mauve towel around her wet hair.

'Don't move, Julia. I'll get it. It's got to be the boys,' Barbie calls out.

Behind the door, she finds Ken and Brad, their arms loaded with packages.

'Hi, Barbie,' Ken says. 'We're a little early, but we were really impatient to see you. We've brought some surprises for you and Julia.'

'Julia's waiting for you in the lounge room,' Barbie says. 'She's just come back from her rehabilitation session. I went for a jog earlier and I've just had a shower. I'll dry my hair and then

I'll be with you. If you want to put the kettle on, I'll make us all some tea in a minute.'

'Hello, boys,' says Julia, comfortably seated on an armchair in the lounge room, her injured leg stretched out before her on a footstool.

'We've found something that we think will interest you,' Brad says. 'This is a video of Katarina skating in a recent competition. She'll be your strongest rival at the Olympic Games. We'll watch the video together. You'll be able to see her strong points and her weaknesses. If you analyse her

skating style, you may be able to perform better than her.'

'What a great idea!' Julia says. 'It's really important to study your fellow competitors if you want to beat them. Well done, boys!'

'Wait until you see what else we brought,' Ken says. 'Can you guess? No? Very well, I'll help you. It's something delicious that you eat.'

'I know! I know!' Barbie shrieks, as she rushes into the lounge room, her long blonde hair flying over her shoulders. She's now dressed in a comfort-

able blue tracksuit. 'I can guess. I think that they're vanilla slices. I love vanilla slices.'

'That's right!' Ken agrees. 'Vanilla slices to eat in front of the TV, while we watch the video.'

While Brad sets up the tape in the video recorder, Barbie and Ken whisper to each other as they prepare the tea in the kitchen.

'What do you think about Julia's progress?' Ken asks. 'Do you think that she'll be able to compete?'

'Christine, her physio, is amazed by her progress, but I

don't know. I'm not sure that she'll be able to perform at her best in time for the Olympic Games. Why are you asking?'

'Simply because we're about to watch Katarina on the video,' Ken replies. 'She's Julia's greatest rival, and I have to tell

you that Katarina is very, very good.'

'Ken, don't worry Julia. We'll just have to wait and see what happens.'

Soon, our four friends are glued to the TV screen watching Katarina's graceful movements. Her black hair is pulled back into a long plait. She wears a blue leotard that has a skirt of blue tulle.

'Her technique is simply brilliant,' Julia says.

'She does beautiful pirouettes, but I don't think her backwards spiral is as good as yours,' Barbie says.

'She always has a frown on her face,' Ken notices. 'It is as if she really isn't that happy to be where she is.'

'She certainly isn't surrounded by friends as wonderful as you are,' Julia says, certain that she has just discovered Katarina's secret flaw.

## Chapter 8

# Katarina's life

Katarina's life is definitely a lot less relaxed than that of our friends. In order to understand what it is like, it is necessary to know a little about her country

and to cast an eye over her coach,
Mr Toumba.

This large man is a mountain
of muscle. As his booming voice
resounds across the skating rink,
Katarina is shaken. Mr Toumba
is not a nasty man, but he is so
keen for his young student to be

successful that he usually forgets to smile.

'Okay, Katarina. We'll have to start again. We have to keep practising until you get it all perfect.'

'But I'm tired, Mr Toumba. I've been skating since eight o'clock this morning. I can't feel my legs any more.'

'What do you mean by that exactly?' Mr Toumba demands. 'That's a very serious thing to say this close to the Olympic Games. Tomorrow, we'll do an extra half-hour of jogging.'

'Oh no!' Katarina says to

herself. 'If I'd known he'd react like that, I wouldn't have said anything.' Furious, she skates off. She picks up so much speed that her next jump is perfectly executed.

'That wasn't bad at all, Katarina,' Mr Toumba says. 'In order to reward you for your effort, I'll give you a half-hour break.'

Delighted by this chance to relax, Katarina unlaces her rollerblades and stumbles into the cafeteria in order to drink some milk and eat a sandwich. Maya, the little gymnast, sits down beside her. She has a glass of orange juice.

'Wow, I'm exhausted!' Katarina says. 'My coach is really pushing me. He wants me to be the best, but I think that all this heavy training will kill me!'

'They're all like that,' Maya says. 'They work us relentlessly. I do three hours of exercises each day at the bar, until I can no longer use my hands. I get cramps, so I have to take little rests.'

'I don't know if athletes in other countries train as hard as we do,' Katarina says. 'I don't think it's possible.'

'We really do train very hard,' Maya agrees. 'But all this training means that we usually get the medals. It's what I dream of.'

'Yes, we all want to be standing in the top position on the podium. Just imagine what it would be like to be there, with a gold medal around your neck as the band plays our national anthem!'

'And as our parents sit in front of the TV and cry with joy!' Maya adds, clapping her hands together.

'Katarina! Katarina!' Mr Toumba calls. 'I said a half-hour break. It's over! Back to work!'

'Oh,' Katarina sighs. 'I've got to go. Thanks, Maya. All this talk of winning medals has made me feel a lot better. Goodbye. Good luck with the rest of your training!'

## Chapter 9

# Ready to depart

The gymnasium is decorated with coloured streamers. In the centre of the room, young women and men dance together to the pounding music. A trestle table has been set up against one wall. It is covered with sandwiches and fruit juices. Balloons hang from the ceiling. Barbie, dressed in a white T-shirt and a hot pink skirt, dances with Ken.

Mick, the team manager, is holding a bottle of champagne. He walks up to Tim. 'Can you

turn down the music for a moment? I've got something I would like to say.'

Tim rushes over to the stereo system to turn down the sound. The dancers, surprised by the interruption, stand frozen on the spot.

'Listen, everyone, please!' Mick says loudly. 'I would like to make a toast to congratulate you on reaching the end of your rigorous training. Please take a glass of champagne each. Tomorrow, the team will fly out for the Olympic Games. Glory awaits you.'

'Hooray!' a lone voice cries out.

'In order to win medals,' Mick continues, 'you will have to beat the finest athletes in the world. But I have confidence in you all. You've worked hard to reach this moment. And you are not alone.

You all have your supporters. Some will be with you, some will be watching on TV.'

'Oh, sir! What about Julia?' a voice calls out. 'Will she be skating?'

'The doctor and her physio are optimistic. In theory, her recovery is going according to plan, but they won't be making any decisions until the very last moment. We will all have to wait and see. If, by chance, Julia cannot participate in the Games, Barbie will replace her. Barbie has been training very hard. They are both champions.'

'For Barbie: hip, hip, hooray!'
Tim yells.

'Hooray!' the crowd shouts in response.

'For Julia: hip, hip, hooray!'
Tim yells again.

'Hooray!' the crowd shouts back.

'And now, more champagne,'
Mick says.

The music is turned back on, and the dancers return to the dance floor.

Julia and Brad walk over to Barbie and Ken.

'Boys,' Julia says, 'Barbie and I are going to need all the

support you can give us. We are starting to get nervous.'

'You've got nothing to worry about,' Ken says. 'We will be right there for you.'

## Chapter 10

# The Olympic Village

The Olympic Village is like a little city within a larger city. There are bungalows within the Village for the athletes to live in. There are shops too, stocked full of mineral water, chocolate, post-cards and newspapers. There are rooms in which to train and nice cafes with terraces, so the athletes can enjoy a drink in the sun.

Julia and Barbie are assigned a bungalow to share. The young women are so exhausted by their flight that they open the door and sink into two large armchairs. The taxi driver who drove them from the airport carries in their suitcases and packages. He places them on the carpeted floor.

On top of an enormous suitcase, sits Joe, the fluffy teddy bear. Julia and Barbie can't do

anything without him by their side. They are certain that the little bear's blue-eyed gaze brings them luck. As Julia trains, Joe sleeps in Barbie's arms. When it is Barbie's turn to enter the rink, she returns the sweet mascot to its owner. Ever since Miss Koper gave Jo to Julia, Jo has not left the arms of our friends.

'When I think I might have for-gotten Jo,' Julia says, looking at the adorable bear.

'I don't think we can forget him, because neither of us can skate without him,' Barbie adds.

'Right now, I think we can safely say that he is sadly observing this messy bungalow. We've brought so much stuff, I don't know where to begin,' Julia says, sighing.

'I'm going to begin by taking a nice, long shower. I'll sort through my luggage after that.'

'I'm going to buy some cold drinks,' Julia says. 'It's so hot in this country.'

A little while later, revitalised and fresh from their showers and drinks, our two skating champions organise the clean-up of their bungalow in record time. Then they decide to go and explore the Olympic Village.

As they walk along the little streets bathed in sunlight, they listen to the people around them speak. All the languages of the world are to be heard here. Barbie and Julia decide to amuse themselves by working out the nationality of their fellow athletes by listening to their accents.

'That big blond guy over there, with the broad shoulders and guttural accent, is Russian, I think,' Barbie says. 'And maybe he's a shot-putter or a hammer thrower. What do you think?'

'You might be right. If he had dark hair, I might think he was Italian, possibly a swimmer.'

'Oh, look!' Barbie cries. 'There's Fanny, our gymnast friend. She and the young girl she's speaking to don't speak the same language.'

'Yes,' Julia laughs, 'I notice that they are trying to speak in a sort of sign language.'

Fanny makes all kinds of gestures as she speaks. She bursts out laughing when she notices that the girl she is speaking to has her eyes wide open and a confused look on her face.

'Hi, Fanny!' Barbie says. 'It looks like you are having trouble explaining things. It must be hard for a chatterbox like you.'

'Hey, be nice, girls,' Fanny says. 'Don't mock me, unless you can speak Russian. Here, I want to introduce you to my greatest rival,

Maya. She's been competing in gymnastics since she was eight years old. She doesn't know a word of our language. Life on this planet would be a lot easier if everyone spoke the same language.'

Barbie and Julia take turns trying to explain to Maya what sport they are here to compete in. When she has finally understood, Maya claps her hands and tells the girls that her best friend is Katrina, the best skater in their country.

'She will be our most difficult competitor,' Julia says, as she lets out a loud sigh.

## Chapter 11

# The opening ceremony

The young women in Barbie's Olympic team are dressed in red and white blouses with a pleated red skirt. The young men wear a similar red and white shirt and red trousers. Everyone wears a little straw boater hat on their head. The hat is decorated with red ribbons. In their ceremonial uniforms, the team members look magnificent. Today is the official opening of the Olympic Games. Thousands of journalists have come from all over the world to observe the ceremony. There are many, many tourists here, supporting their teams. Yesterday afternoon, Julia and Barbie went to their airport to meet Ken, Brad, Skipper and the bulk of their fan club.

The stadium seating is filled

with sports lovers. The immense crowd begins to feel impatient as they wait for the parade of athletes to begin.

Suddenly, the large doors open and the orchestra of the Games enters, moving to the beat

of the music they are playing. Following them, smartly organised behind their countries' flags, come the teams. Each time the athletes pass a group of their admirers, there is a mighty wave of applause.

'I'm so nervous,' Julia whispers, as she marches alongside Barbie.

'It will be worse when we are standing alone on the rink,' Barbie replies softly.

Once they have done a round of the stadium, the athletes arrange themselves in the lawn in the centre. By chance, Barbie and Julia find themselves in the very front row, well placed to see the opening spectacle in its entirety. As the last athletes settle on the lawn, a waiting silence fills the stadium.

Suddenly, a deep voice echoes around the field. It's the Prime Minister. He is on a stage in the middle of the lawn. In a very sombre tone, he pronounces the opening of the Olympic Games.

Trumpets resound loudly, quickly followed by the official song of the Games. Once more the doors of the stadium open, and a young sprinter brandishing the Olympic flame bursts into the stadium. The crowd roars with awe and excitement. The sprinter climbs up huge steps until he reaches a large basin in which he places the flame. As the stadium flame is lit, the crowd shouts happily. The stadium vibrates from the loud shouts

and applause. A dozen white doves are released from cages on the lawn. They take flight and disappear into the sky.

When the crowd is silent once more, an athlete steps on to the stage. She stands before the microphone and recites the

Olympic pledge on behalf of all the athletes.

Then the entertainment begins. Dancers begin a winding, spectacular ballet. They are joined by musicians and acrobats who are dressed in colourful costumes. The night is fine and clear. Stars twinkle in the sky. It is magical.

Later at supper, Barbie and her friends speak of the ceremony they have just taken part in.

'It was amazing!' Brad says.

'I've never seen anything so beautiful in my whole life,' Skipper confesses.

'During the recitation of the pledge, my heart was going at a million miles an hour,' Barbie says.

'I never imagined that taking part in the opening ceremony would be so moving,' Julia admits.

'It is great to see athletes from different countries brought together by their love of sport,' Ken says. 'I imagine that all the world's people were united tonight in brotherhood.'

'That's a wonderful thing to say,' Julia says. 'It will be poss-ible, one day.'

'It's sport that brings people together,' Barbie says. 'Whether you are swimming or running together, climbing or dancing together, you don't need to speak the same language. I think that's an incredible thing.'

'Yes, so, after having had such a lovely day, shall we now return home?' Julia asks mischievously.

'Go home? Have you lost your mind?' one member of the fan club cries.

'There's one more wonder we haven't seen yet,' another fan says, 'the medals. And we won't be returning home without them.'

Chapter 12

# The diving competition

Lisa is standing on the top of the diving tower. From below, she seems small and terribly fragile. She is at the base of the diving board, concentrating hard. She

92

walks up to the end of the board and the crowd around the pool holds its breath.

Lisa prepares to jump. Her feet are together and she raises on to her toes. Suddenly, she lifts her arms high, bounces on the board and leaps into the air. She forms a succession of whirls, swirls and somersaults as she dives. At the moment her hands touch the water in the pool, her legs are completely straight and aligned. She enters the water without a splash. She made it looks so easy. She emerges from the water and waits by the pool to find out the scores that the judges have awarded her.

The scores appear on the scoreboard. They are excellent. Everyone applauds.

'I thought that was fantastic!' Barbie exclaims, happy to support her friend. Julia and the boys agree.

'When she dove into the pool, it was so clean and neat,' Ken says.

'The next diver is her main competitor,' Julia says. 'It's Kim, the young Chinese woman. She's amazing. In my opinion, it won't be easy for the judges to decide between the two of them.'

'It won't be long before we know the result,' Barbie says. 'This is their last dive.'

The divers climb up the diving tower. Kim will dive first. Some of the other divers are obviously nervous and anxious. Some of them flex their hands and arms in preparation. Other girls rub their thighs to warm them. Often the divers who get low scores are the ones who enter the water too violently, making a large splash as they hit the water.

Finally, it is time for Kim's last dive. Balancing on the very edge of the diving board, Kim takes a deep breath. Then, in a swift action, she bounces and dives into a series of twists, but she enters the water before she is able to bring her legs back together. There is a big splash.

'That was not a great dive!' Barbie cries. 'That will be very good for Lisa.'

Now Lisa stands on the diving board. She bounces and leaps, arms outstretched, and looks like a bird taking flight. She performs a series of dizzying twists before she enters the water perfectly and precisely. The crowd cheers. No other diver will be able to beat

that dive. The final score is inevitable.

A little while later, Lisa steps on to the podium to receive her gold medal. Barbie calls out to her, 'Bravo, bravo, Lisa! You're our first gold medallist.'

'In my opinion, she won't be the last,' Ken murmurs into Barbie's ear.

## Chapter 13

# The gymnastics competition

Since their arrival at the Olympic Village, Barbie and Julia have trained very hard. Their training sessions have prevented them from seeing the main part of the gymnastics competition in which their little friend Fanny has been competing. The young women learn that Fanny has won on the beam and also in the individual division. They know that in the team event, their country is well placed. Barbie and Julia really want to watch Fanny compete in the rhythmic gymnastics competition this afternoon. So all morning, the young women train very hard. They want to impress Miss Koper so they can ask her to give them the afternoon off.

'Your event is in three days.

I'm not sure that I should let you have the afternoon off,' Miss Koper says.

'I promise you that we'll work extra hard tomorrow morning. At the moment, Fanny is very nervous. We know that our presence will reassure her. You understand that, don't you, Miss Koper?' Barbie pleads.

'Yes, I understand. I understand,' their coach agrees. 'Let's make the most of this session then. Barbie, we'll begin with the backwards spin.'

As Barbie and Julia train, the young men occupy themselves

with a picnic. Finally, at two
o'clock, everyone finds themselves in the gymnasium, with its
gleaming wooden floors. All the
competitors are busy preparing
themselves for the challenge
ahead.

'Thank you so much for

coming,' Fanny says, as soon as she sees her friends. 'I'm completely scared to death, because during the warm up one of the other competitors kept giving me filthy looks. It's as though she hates me. I get anxious just passing her in the corridors.'

'I'd take it as a good sign, Fanny,' Barbie says. 'It shows that she is nervous around you, probably because she fears your ability. Next time you see her, tell yourself that she is more scared of you than you are of her. She knows that you are very talented and she's just trying to unsettle you by glaring at you. Don't fall into her trap!'

'Are you sure that's why she keeps giving me such cold, arrogant looks?' Fanny asks.

'I'm certain of it. I've often noticed that people have that attitude when they are jealous or worried. You've got no need to intimidate your competition in the same way because you are a better gymnast than they are. I've no doubt you'll win this afternoon's event.'

'Good!' Fanny says, feeling relieved. 'Your arrival was well timed, Barbie. We should make you the team psychologist. You are such a help to your teammates! Thanks to you, I feel much calmer and stronger. I'm sure I can win now. I better go and line up.'

While Barbie, Julia, Skipper and the boys enjoy some popcorn, the gymnastics competitors officially enter the room. They are dressed in lovely costumes and they carry the ribbons they will use during their routines. Some of the girls somersault or spin into the gymnasium. The moment that Fanny appears in the room, the packets of popcorn disappear under the seats. To support Fanny, Barbie and her friends need to concentrate on her performance.

Fanny is the last to perform. No one has ever seen such a brilliant routine before. As Fanny comes to the end of her routine, she leaps into the air. Her ribbon twirls high above her head. Fanny ends her leap with a somersault.

A little while later, Fanny climbs on to the podium. The judges and the spectators give her a standing ovation. The entire

gymnasium reverberates with the sound of mighty applause. As Fanny receives her gold medal, her friends cheer and cry with unbridled joy.

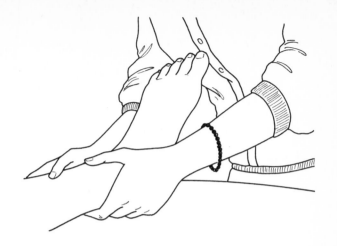

## Chapter 14

# Barbie or Julia?

Lying on the massage table, Julia gives herself up to Christine's strong hands. Christine, Julia's physio, is massaging Julia's sore ankle.

'Christine, do you think I am going to be able to compete?' Julia asks. 'I feel up to it.'

'Well, I think that you have recovered extremely well,' Christine replies. 'And if it was up to me to decide whether you'll be competing, I would say yes. However, your doctor is a little more cautious than I am, and she must make the final decision. She may want you to rest for a bit longer before you enter a com-petition.'

'But I don't understand why,' Julia says. 'My training sessions have all gone very well.'

'Every day that she trains, Julia gets better and better,' Barbie says, as she enters the room.

'But you have been making great progress, too,' Christine says. 'I think that the doctor might prefer to see you compete, rather

than have Julia run the risk of doing more damage to her ankle. I will speak up for you, Julia, but it's not only my opinion that counts. The doctor's opinion is very important, too.'

'And who in the end will make the final decision?' Barbie asks. 'Miss Koper? The doctor? You? The team manager?'

'Tomorrow, we'll be discussing the issue together and we'll make the decision that we feel is best for everyone.'

'You must know that it's pretty hard for Julia and me right now. The competition is only two days away and we don't know who will be competing,' Barbie says.

'I don't doubt that, Barbie,' Christine agrees, 'but tomorrow, I promise you, you'll have an answer.'

The next day, the doctor examines Julia closely. The doctor then has a private meeting with Miss Koper, Christine and Mick.

During this time, on the other side of the door, Barbie and Julia stand waiting. They bite their nails with nervousness.

'The suspense is horrible,' Barbie says. 'I can't wait for the

door to open, so we can finally hear the decision.'

'We've both been training so hard,' Julia says. 'How will they choose?'

Brad, Ken, Skipper and members of the fan club come to give the young women their support.

'We'll support you both, no matter what the outcome of the meeting is,' Ken says. 'We've brought some refreshments to help pass the time.'

Everyone chats. They are trying to distract Barbie and Julia to help calm them down.

Suddenly the door opens. Miss Koper pops her head out. 'Barbie? Julia? If you could step inside, please.'

'Oh, Miss, can we come, too?' asks one of the fan club members.

'If you want to,' Miss Koper says. 'Come on in.'

'Julia and Barbie,' Mick, the team manager, says. 'Thank you for being so patient while we made our decision. We all think that Julia is in good enough form to compete, so she will compete in the Games. But we think that it would be unfair to Barbie if all her hard work and training came to nothing, so we have decided to enter Barbie in the competition as well. This way, we are doubling our chances for a medal. Are you happy with the decision?'

'Yes! Yippee!' Julia and Barbie yell together, as they jump up and down.

'Yay!' cry their friends. 'We have a great chance of winning gold now. Hooray for Barbie and Julia.'

## Chapter 15

# The hour of truth

The night before the competition, the two young women do not sleep well. Overcome by nerves and the knowledge that tomorrow is the big day, they cannot fall asleep. Finally in the early hours of the morning, completely exhausted, they both fall into a deep sleep.

They are still in bed when Miss Koper bursts into their bungalow at seven o'clock in the morning. Sweetly, she boils the kettle to make them some tea to have with their breakfast. She finishes by opening the curtains in the bedrooms. This way, the sun will wake up her two pupils.

Barbie and Julia join Miss Koper in the kitchen.

'We're so grateful for your help today, Miss Koper,' Barbie says.

'I'll take care of all the small things, so that you can both stay focused on this morning's competition,' Miss Koper replies. 'It's important that you're ready to skate at eleven o'clock.'

'Good gracious! The hour of truth is approaching,' Julia cries.

After their breakfast, Barbie

and Julia spend an hour exercising and stretching. Stressed yet confident, Miss Koper holds Jo while her students train. She knows that Jo is an important mascot for both young women.

'You won't forget to bring Jo to the rink, will you?' Julia asks.

'Seeing him gives us confidence,' Barbie adds.

At precisely ten o'clock, the two young women enter the competitors' changing room near the skating rink. They slip into their leotards for the competition. Barbie is wearing a white leotard with a silver star pattern and a skirt. Julia is wearing a pale green leotard with a skirt. They apply make-up to make their eyes and lips stand out. They look professional and beautiful, but their hearts are beating quickly.

'We've got to forget about the audience watching us,' Barbie

says to Julia. 'But on the other hand, we don't want to disappoint our fans. We want to win for them.'

As it is only a demonstration sport at these Olympic Games, the rollerblading competition will take place in a single trial. Barbie and Julia do not want to get distracted before the competition, so they wait in the changing room.

Julia will skate before Barbie. When she hears her name, she throws her arms around Barbie.

'Go on,' Barbie says. 'I'll be with you. I'll stand at the side of the rink to encourage you. Good luck. You will be wonderful!'

And Julia is wonderful! During the four minutes of her routine, the members of the audience are breathless as they watch her. The judges' high scores place her in the top position. Completely exhausted but delighted with her perform-ance, Julia takes her place on the bench as Barbie is called. Barbie moves gracefully into the centre of the rink.

The music begins and Barbie starts her routine. She does pirouettes and swirls, and she

leaps into the air. All of her steps are executed with such precision that she makes rollerblading appear effortless. Near the end of her routine, Barbie leaps into a fast pirouette. Her long blonde hair covers her face and the skirt of her leotard stretches out to look like a flower. As the music stops, so does Barbie. She feels the ground tremble as the audience applauds. All the judges award her very high scores, which place her first, just in front of Julia.

While it looks good for our friends, Katarina has yet to perform and she is the current world champion.

## Chapter 16

# The party

Katarina skates onto the rink. She is wearing a leotard decorated with ostrich feathers. Everyone applauds. Katarina is breathing quickly. It is obvious that she is a little anxious. She is nervous because she is the current world champion and she has just watched Barbie and Julia perform. She knows that in order to win, she must perform at her best. She must take risks.

The music starts out very slow and tender. Katarina appears to

be transported elsewhere by the music. She moves slowly, looking like a little bird balancing in the wind. As they watch her move with ease and grace, Julia and Barbie, sitting on their bench, tremble. They know that a good performance by Katarina will put her in first place.

The second part of Katarina's performance is faster. The music is rock and roll. Always in time with the beat, Katarina's moves become more elaborate and her jumps become faster. Yet when she lands after one jump, she wavers a little. It looks like she might fall, but she doesn't, but she is no longer in time with the music. She quickly finishes her routine and there is a strained look on her face. She does not smile. She knows she has not done well.

The judges saw the little stumble. Their scores reflect their loss of confidence in her. Katarina takes third place behind Barbie and Julia.

Glued to their seats with shock, the two young women can hardly believe their eyes.

'Julia, we've won!' Barbie screams. 'Katarina did not perform as well as us. We got the

gold and silver medals! We won!'
'I can't believe it, Barbie! It's too
good to be true!'

The crowd is on its feet,
congratulating the best rollerbladers in the world. Barbie and
Julia fall into each other's arms.
They are both in tears.

'I'm so happy that you got the gold medal, Barbie, because without you, I would never have had the courage to start training so hard again.'

'I can say for sure that without you, I would never have begun this crazy journey. We are both champions!'

Later, when they step up on to the podium, Barbie and Julia pat Katarina on the back as she takes third place.

That evening, Katarina comes to a sumptuous party organised by Skipper and the fan club. The party is in honour of the medal winners in the Olympic roller-blading demonstration.

For the first time, the young woman seems intimidated. Unused to easy displays of tenderness and joy, she is shocked when the young men and women dance and laugh together. Even though Katarina does not speak the same language as her new friends, it is not too much of a handicap as she hangs out with Barbie and Julia. Little by little, she gains more confidence. She bursts into laughter when Barbie presents her with Jo, the fluffy teddy bear mascot. At the end of the night, it's Katarina who leads the group in a mad dance.

Just before it is time to leave, Ken gives Barbie a hug. He whispers into her ear, 'I'm terribly proud of you, and I have something for you.' He sweetly

slides a necklace around Barbie's neck. 'Your medal will be too heavy to wear every day. I want you to accept this necklace as a symbol of what you have achieved here.'

'And now, for some toasts!' Julia cries. 'Everyone, raise your glasses. Miss Koper, thank you for all your hard work and advice!'

But Miss Koper isn't listening. She is deep in conversation with Mr Toumba, Katarina's trainer.

'What champions those two would train if they married,' Barbie says to Ken.

'To the most beautiful medal-lists of the Olympic Games!' Tim cries. 'For Barbie, Julia and Katarina: hip, hip, hooray!'

'To all of you who gave us so much support: hip, hip, hooray!' replies Barbie, as she raises her glass.

*The end*

# Other titles in this series: